characters created by

lauren child

We
honestly
CAN look after
your dog

PUFFIN

Charlie and Lola™

Text based on script written by Bridget Hurst and Carol Noble

Illustrations from

the TV animation

produced by Tiger Aspect

PUFFIN BOOKS
Published by the Penguin Group: London, New York, Australia,
Canada, India, Ireland, New Zealand and South Africa
Penguin Books Ltd, Registered Offices: 80 Strand, London WC2R 0RL, England

puffinbooks.com

First published in Puffin Books 2005
This edition published 2012
001 – 10 9 8 7 6 5 4 3 2 1
Text and illustrations copyright © Lauren Child/Tiger Aspect Productions Limited, 2005
Charlie and Lola word and logo ® and © Lauren Child, 2005
Charlie and Lola is produced by Tiger Aspect Productions
Made and printed in China
ISBN (pack): 978-0-718-19386-7

I have this little sister Lola.
She is small and very funny.
At the moment Lola really, really wants to have a dog.
But Mum and Dad say she can't because our flat
is too small and Lola is too young to look after one.

Lola says,
"Say **woof**, Charlie."

So I say,
"Woof."

Then Lola says, "**Sit!**"

So I sit.

My
cereal
bowl
is
now
a **dog** bowl.

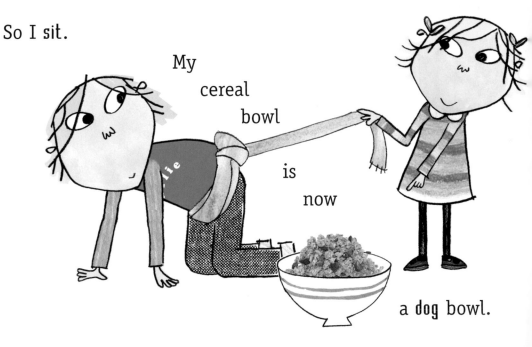

And she has made me a **dog** bed.

Lola just loves **dogs**.

A lot.

One day Dad took us to the park.

There was me and my friend Marv,
Lola and her friend Lotta.
And Sizzles.
Sizzles is Marv's **dog**.

Lola loves Sizzles.

So does Lola's best friend, Lotta.

Lola says, "You ask."
Lotta says, "No you ask."

So Lola says,
"Marv, can we look after Sizzles?"

Marv says,
       "Lola, do you know
about dogs?"

Lola says,
"Yes I do. Everything."

And Lotta says, "So do I."

Lola says,

"We know that Sizzles is a very extremely very clever dog. We know he can do very good tricks."

Lotta says, "If he wanted he could roll over."

Lola says,
"And dance.
Definitely, I think.
Lotta, do you know
I think
Sizzles
can do
really
anything."

Lola says,
"And
walk
on
two
legs."

Lotta says,
"And speak English."

While Marv is trying to
make Sizzles sit, I see some of our
friends playing football
and I think I'd really like to play too.

So I say,
"We could play just one game,
Marv?"

Marv says,
"But who is going to look after
Sizzles?"

Lola says, "Me!"

Lotta says, "Me!"

I say,
"It is only for a little while.
He'll be OK with Lola and Lotta.
I'm pretty sure he will."

So Marv says,
        "OK.
        But you do know that
there are lots of **rules**
        if you want to
                look after Sizzles.

No **chocolates.**

Or **cakes.**

And
        no **sweets**
of **any** kind.

Completely
no digging...

and

no chasing birds.

And

no

s p l a s h i n g

in

puddles.

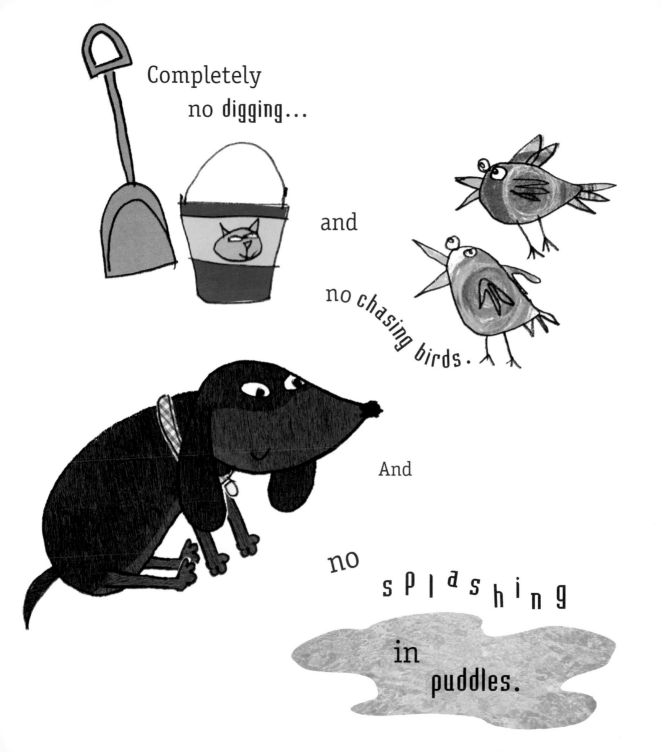

And
NO
taking him
off the
lead."

Marv says,
    "Do you honestly promise to
look after my dog?"

            Lola says, "Honestly,
        we do promise honestly,
                to look after your dog."

Lotta says,
    "Honestly and promisedly, we do."

Lola says,
"Dogs must be stroked and patted."

Lotta says,
"To tell them we're their friend."

Lola says,
"Playing... is
    what makes dogs happy."

Lotta says,
"And grooming makes dogs feel pretty."

Lola says,
    "Dogs must go outside
and must walk."

Lotta says,
    "Otherwise what is the point
of their legs?"

Then Lola says,
"Lotta, I don't think you really know
all about dogs like me."

And Lotta says,
"Lola, I really do know
everything about dogs."

Lola says, "But Lotta, I'm in charge."

And Lotta says,
"So am I."

Lola says,

"We're both in charge, but I think that Mary said that I was a little bit more in charge than you.

"You see, Lotta, you must hold the lead like this. See?" Lotta says, "Oh no, Lola. You really must do it like this."

"Oh no!"

"Sizzles, where are you?"

"Where are you, Sizzles?"

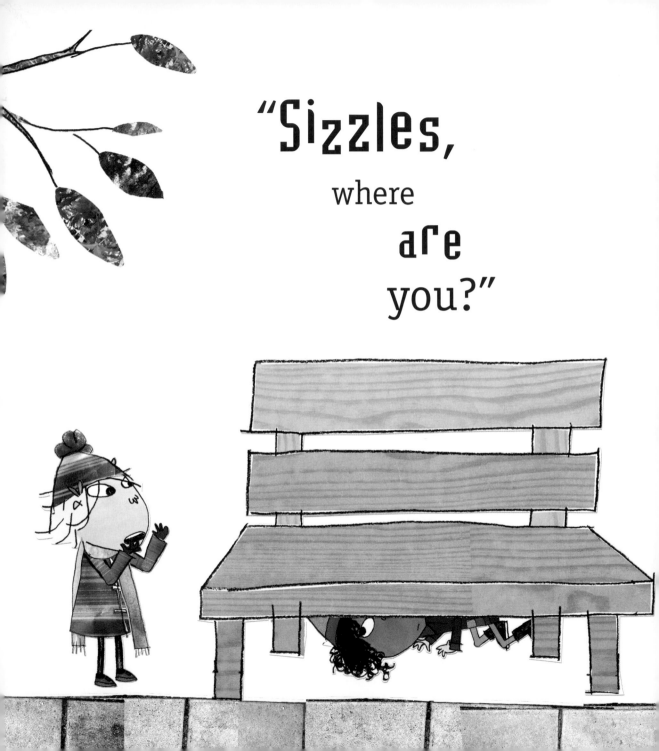

"Sizzles,
where
are
you?"

Lola says,
    "Do you think we have
lost him **forever**?"

        Lotta says,
    "I think he was **sad** actually."

            Then Lola says...

"Sizzles!"

But then Lola says,
"Oh no! There are two Sizzleses!"

And Lotta says,
"No, Lola, there are two dogs.
But only one is Sizzles."

Lola says,
"But which one?"

Lotta says,
"I don't know."

Lola says,
"The clever one!
Sizzles can do anything, remember?"

Lotta says, "Yes. Sizzles can do anything...

... Sizzles can sit!

Sizzles! Sit. Sit. Sit!"

And Lola says,
"Sit. Sit. Please sit!"

Lotta says,
"Sit, sit, sit.
Will you sit!"

Then Lola says,
"Sizzles! It's Sizzles!"

When me and Marv finished playing football,
we went to find Lola and Lotta.
I say, "Come on, you two. It's time to go."

But Lola and Lotta look a bit fidgety.

And they both whisper,
"Charlie, we had Sizzles
and we were
looking after him..."

then he sort of went for a walk...

without his lead.
        And then we couldn't see him any more.
        And then we saw him but he wasn't one,
he was two Sizzleses.

        And so... I'm not sure

        that Sizzles
            is
        Sizzles now."

So I say, "Look here! Dog number: 144. Sizzles.
Owner: Marv Lowe,
5a Crocodile Street."

Then Marv says,
"That's his dog tag. It's got his name and address on it,
in case he gets lost.

All dogs have them."

And Lola says,
"We knew that actually, Marv."

And Lotta says,
"Just in case
they get lost."

I say,
"Yes, that's right.
Just in case
they get
lost!"

And Lola says, "But Sizzles would **never** get lost."
Lotta says, "Because he's **very clever**."
Lola says, "He can do **absolutely anything**."
And Marv says, "Come on, Sizzles, we're going home."